SANTA'S WONDERFUL WORKSHOP

ELYS DOLAN

OXFORD
UNIVERSITY PRESS

For Holly and Pete – E.D.

OXFORD
UNIVERSITY PRESS

Great Clarendon Street, Oxford OX2 6DP

Oxford is a registered trade mark of
Oxford University Press in the UK and in certain other countries

Text and illustrations copyright © Elys Dolan 2018

Data available

ISBN: 978-0-19-274617-7 (paperback)

1 3 5 7 9 10 8 6 4 2

Printed in China

CHRISTMAS DAY

Hi, I'm Santa and I've just got back from delivering the presents. We did an excellent job this year, but the elves say next year is going to be the busiest yet.

Luckily, I've got everything under control . . .

Mr Johnson from next door is very angry about the noise,
but I'm sure the penguins will calm down soon . . .

MARCH

The penguin situation is getting out of hand. I've asked Barry the Bauble Co-ordinator to help the penguins settle in.

APRIL

With Barry in charge of the penguins, I've had time
to join the reindeer's dance troop.

MAY

But maybe I should have been keeping a closer eye on the elves.
I'm not entirely convinced by their new creations . . .

JUNE

The PRESENT-O-MATIC machine has started making toasters. Yes, TOASTERS! We didn't even know it could make them. I can't think what's causing it.

I'm sure the engineering elves will fix
things. I'll just keep calm, stay jolly,
and eat another candy cane.

JULY

We'd just got the PRESENT-O-MATIC working again when the heating broke. This shouldn't be a problem in summer, but when you live in the North Pole, trust me, it is.

I love what you've done with the place!

The pipes are gone. It's going to cost you.

Has anyone seen a bear?

Bath-toy testing has come to a standstill and most of the elves are frozen.

AUGUST

After the big freeze, everyone has flu.
Doctor Frostihands says we'll all have to stay in
bed and catch up on work when we're better.

SEPTEMBER

But I've decided we all need a holiday. It's been a busy year.
Plus, I can catch up with old friends.

NOVEMBER

I bailed out the elves from the police station
and Holly convinced the reindeer to lend a hand.

DECEMBER

It's almost Christmas
Eve! We should be
getting some rest
before the big
night, but I just
can't say no to
snowballs.

We're in a big rush to finish the presents now,
so I'm sure they'll be very helpful . . .

At least the sleigh is packed and ready.

CHRISTMAS EVE

Tonight is the night! We've made the presents, wrapped them, and the reindeer are ready to go. Time to deliver!

But wait a minute. Holly is acting a bit weird . . .

There is only one thing to do . . .

Sometimes when you're the boss you have to take charge.

But then, Holly has a great idea. If we all work together, we might just pull it off.

Later that night, we all get down to work.

No, not there! Oh fine.

And we carry out Holly's plan just in time for . . . **CHRISTMAS DAY!**

Oh dear.

My vase!

Don't touch that!

Well, there you go. The children are happy, the penguins are happy, and no one got eaten by a bear.

Holly says there will be even more children next year. But if
we all stick together, I'm sure everything will be fine.
I mean, what else could possibly go wrong?

Wait a minute . . . WHAT DID WE DO
WITH THAT BEAR?

Can I stay
another year?